Max and Mama

Laura Numeroff

Illustrated by Masha Sudovykh

© 2025 Laura Numeroff

All rights reserved. No part of this book may be used or reproduced
in any manner without written permission except in the case
of brief quotations embodied in critical articles or reviews.

This is a work of fiction. Any similarity to real persons,
living or dead, is coincidental and not intended by the author.

Max and Mama

Michael Sampson Books
Dallas / New York
www.MichaelSampsonBooks.com
(972) 381-0009

A New Era in Publishing®

Publisher's Cataloging-In-Publication Data

Names: Numeroff, Laura Joffe, author. | Sudovykh, Masha, illustrator.
Title: Max and Mama / Laura Numeroff ; illustrated by Masha Sudovykh.
Description: Dallas ; New York : Michael Sampson Books, [2025] | Interest age level: 004-008.
| Summary: Max and Mama are spending the day together! A delicious breakfast, a game of hide-and-seek, and a picnic at the park. But as they ride their bikes home, one of Max's training wheels falls off--suddenly, this special day has a whole new adventure for Max and Mama to tackle!--Publisher.
Identifiers: ISBN: 978-1-61254-689-6 (hardcover) | LCCN: 2024947404
Subjects: LCSH: Dogs--Juvenile fiction. | Mother and child--Juvenile fiction. | Cycling--Juvenile fiction. | CYAC: Dogs--Fiction. | Mother and child--Fiction. | Bicycles and bicycling--Fiction. | LCGFT: Action and adventure fiction. | BISAC: JUVENILE FICTION / Animals / Dogs. | JUVENILE FICTION / Family / General.
Classification: LCC: PZ7.N964 Ma 2025 | DDC: [E]--dc23

This book has been officially leveled by using the
F&P Text Level Gradient™ Leveling System.

ISBN 978-1-61254-689-6
LCCN 2024947404

Printed in China
10 9 8 7 6 5 4 3 2 1

To contact the author, please go to
www.LauraNumeroff.com.

For more information, please go to
www.MichaelSampsonBooks.com.

For Tom—
Thank you for a truly wonderful experience!
—**Laura Numeroff**

For Alfie—
The very best boy who made me a dog person forever.
—**Masha Sudovykh**

One Sunday morning, Max woke up and got dressed.

Mama helped him put on his favorite sweater.

She made delicious blueberry pancakes for breakfast.

When they
finished eating,
Max and Mama gave
Papa a wave good-bye.

They rode their
bicycles to the park.

Max couldn't wait to play
hide-and-seek.

Max was very

good at hiding.

After riding around the lake,
they stopped at their favorite picnic spot.

Mama spread out a blanket and they
munched on strawberries, biscuits,
and baby carrots.

Max told Mama about the science project his class was working on at school.

After lunch, they took a nap.

Then they headed for home.

Suddenly, one of Max's training wheels broke off!

"Oh, no!" cried Max.

"Can you fix it?" Max asked.

"I don't think I can fix it here," Mama said. "What do you want to do, Max?"

"I think . . ."

"We could walk our bikes home," Mama said.

". . . I think I want to try riding without my training wheels," Max replied.

Max took a deep breath and gave it a try.

Right away, he crashed into some bushes!

"Oops!" he said, brushing himself off and fixing his helmet.

Max got back on his bike. This time, he rode a little further before he wobbled, and fell onto the grass.

Mama asked, "Do you want to take a break?"

"No!" said Max. "I want to try again!"

This time, he rode a little faster, and quickly got the hang of it!

"Look, Mama! No training wheels!"

As soon as they got home, Max told Papa all about their day.

Papa was so proud to hear that he could ride without his training wheels!

Max helped Mama make soup for dinner.

After they ate, Mama helped Max with his science homework.

Then it was time for a bubble bath.

Max loved making shampoo horns.

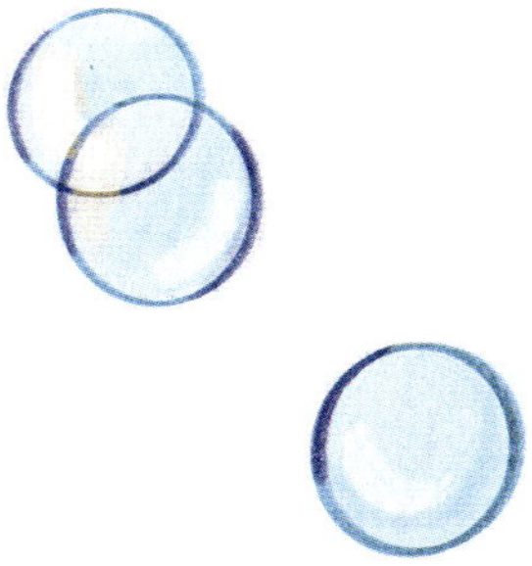

Once Max was nice and clean, he put on his jammies and brushed his teeth.

Then he picked out some books
and made himself cozy in bed.

When Mama finished reading to him,
she gave Max a kiss good-night.

As Max closed his eyes he said,
"I can't wait to ride my bike tomorrow."

Laura Numeroff is the acclaimed #1 *New York Times* bestselling children's author of *If You Give a Mouse a Cookie* and the subsequent If You Give series. Born and raised in Brooklyn, New York, Laura grew up surrounded by art, music, and books. She graduated from Pratt Institute in 1975 with a BFA with honors and a contract from Macmillan for her first children's book. Since then, she has published forty-eight books, and continues to write.

Laura has visited over one hundred schools, numerous children's hospitals, and has virtually visited schools in Germany, Japan, Italy, China, and Colombia. She donates a portion of her book royalties to First Book, a nonprofit organization that provides brand-new books to children in underserved communities, and recently worked with Village Book Builders to fund a brand-new library at a school in Malawi.

Laura now resides in Los Angeles, California, with her dog, Eloise, and her cat, Henry.

Masha Sudovykh is an illustrator primarily focused on children's books, with over fifteen titles to her name. Her work spans a range of projects, from picture books to chapter books to book covers. Masha's illustrations invite readers to find joy in small moments, making her work both relatable and endearing. She draws inspiration from classic children's literature and the everyday life around her.

Having recently moved across the world, Masha now calls Toronto home, where she lives with her partner (and, shockingly, no dog as of yet!). She spends her time cooking, bird-watching, and working on her next exciting picture book.